CHIEF OF WAR

A Critical Companion to the Epic
Hawaiian Series

By

Debbie Barnes

Table of Content

Picture this: it's August 1, 2025, and Apple TV+ is about to drop Chief of War, a nine-episode epic that's got Jason Momoa's name plastered all over it—star, co-creator, and probably the guy who carried the cameras to set. The trailer alone, with its lush Hawaiian vistas and Momoa's intense stare, promises a gritty dive into 19th-century Hawaii, where cultural clashes and power struggles take center stage. But does this ambitious series live up to the hype, or is it just another streaming giant flexing its budget muscles? Buckle up, because we're about to unpack this beast without spilling any plot beans.

In this review, we'll slice through Chief of War like a machete through sugarcane, covering six angles: the plot and themes that drive the story, the star power of Momoa and his co-stars, the direction and jaw-dropping cinematography, the music that sets the mood, the behind-the-scenes production hustle, and its streaming potential in a crowded market. Expect sharp analysis, a few chuckles, and some hard questions about whether this show earns its place in your watchlist. By the end, we'll wrap it up with a verdict on who'll eat this up and a score out of 10. Let's dive into the Hawaiian heart of Chief of War and see if it's a triumph or a tropical misfire.

Chapter 1

Plot and Themes – A Hawaiian Epic with Heart and Heat

When you fire up the trailer for Chief of War, Apple TV+'s nine-episode saga set to drop on August 1, 2025, you're hit with a wave of visuals that scream ambition: lush Hawaiian jungles, warriors wielding spears, and Jason Momoa's brooding glare promising something big. But what's the story here, and what's it trying to say? Without spilling any plot twists—because, let's be real, I haven't seen the full show yet, and I'm not about to ruin your binge—the trailer and early buzz give us plenty to chew on. Chief of War is a historical drama rooted in late 18th-century Hawaii, a time when the islands were a cultural and political powder keg. It's a story about power, identity, and survival, wrapped in a package that's as much about heart as it is about heat.

From what we can glean, the plot centers on a native Hawaiian warrior—played by Momoa, naturally—who's navigating the unification of the islands under a single ruler. The trailer hints at a clash between tradition and change, with tribal leaders, foreign influences, and internal rivalries all vying for control. Think Game of Thrones meets The

Last of the Mohicans, but with a distinctly Hawaiian soul. The story seems to follow Momoa's character as he balances loyalty to his people with the brutal realities of leadership and warfare. There's talk of alliances, betrayals, and sacrifices, all set against a backdrop of a culture fighting to preserve itself while the world creeps in. It's not just swords and shouting matches; the trailer suggests a deeper thread about what it means to be Hawaiian at a turning point in history.

The themes here are meaty, and the show doesn't seem shy about digging into them. First up is identity—personal and cultural.

The trailer's shots of sacred rituals and ancestral lands scream a story about holding onto who you are when outside forces (hello, colonial powers) start knocking. Momoa, who's also a co-creator, has been vocal on X about wanting to tell a Hawaiian story from a native perspective, and that authenticity seems baked into the premise. You can feel the tension between preserving tradition and adapting to survive, a universal struggle that hits harder when it's tied to a specific culture's history. There's also a strong vibe of leadership under pressure—think less "heroic king" and more "guy who's got the weight of his people on his shoulders and might crack." The trailer's quick cuts of battles and quiet moments of reflection suggest a story that's as much about inner turmoil as it is about external conflict.

But let's not get too starry-eyed. Big themes can sometimes trip over themselves if the writing doesn't deliver. The trailer's heavy on visuals—sweeping shots of volcanoes, intense war cries—but light on dialogue, which makes me wonder if the script can match the spectacle. Will the show lean too hard on Momoa's charisma to carry the story, or will it give us layered characters and a plot that doesn't just coast on "epic" vibes? Historical dramas can fall into the trap of feeling like a history lesson rather than a living, breathing story, and I'm hoping Chief of War avoids that. The Hawaiian setting is a fresh change from the usual medieval castles or dusty Westerns, but it's gotta earn its emotional punches. If it's just "badass warrior does badass things," it risks feeling like a pretty postcard with no soul.

Another theme that pops is family—not just blood ties, but the broader idea of community. The trailer shows glimpses of village life, elders, and kids, hinting that the stakes aren't just about who wins the next battle but about what's left for the next generation. This could be the show's secret weapon, grounding the big, bloody conflicts in something relatable. But there's a fine line between heartfelt and hokey, and I'm crossing my fingers the writers don't lean on clichés like the noble warrior's tearful speech to rally the troops. The early buzz on X suggests Momoa's pushing for authenticity, drawing from Hawaiian oral histories, which is promising. If the show can weave those cultural details into a tight, character-driven plot, it might just be the kind of story that sticks with you long after the credits roll.

So, what's the vibe? Chief of War is shaping up to be a bold swing at a historical epic with a Hawaiian heart, tackling identity, leadership, and community in a way that feels both specific and universal. It's got the potential to be a knockout, but it's walking a tightrope between profound and predictable. The trailer's got me hooked, but I'm keeping one eyebrow raised until I see if the story can match the scenery.

Chapter 2

The Movie's Stars – Momoa and the Crew Bringing Hawaii to Life

When you think Chief of War, the first name that pops is Jason Momoa. The guy's a human tsunami, and in this Apple TV+ series, he's not just the lead—he's a co-creator, producer, and probably the dude who made sure the craft services table had enough Spam musubi. But a show this big can't ride on one man's chiseled jawline alone, no matter how iconic. So, who's carrying the weight of this late 18th-century Hawaiian saga, and do they have the chops to make it sing? Let's break down the star power, from Momoa's larger-than-life presence to the ensemble around him, and see if this cast can turn Chief of War into a must-watch or if they're just along for the tropical ride.

Jason Momoa is the beating heart of this show, and the trailer makes that clear in about three seconds. Playing a native Hawaiian warrior leading his people through a turbulent era, he's all intensity—those furrowed brows and battle-ready snarls are pure Momoa, dialed to 11. The man's no stranger to commanding the screen, whether he's swinging a trident as

Aquaman or brooding as Khal Drogo in Game of Thrones. Here, he's in his element, not just because he's Hawaiian himself but because he's got a personal stake in telling this story right. X posts from fans and Momoa himself highlight his passion for showcasing Hawaiian culture, and you can feel that authenticity in the trailer's fleeting moments of him chanting or staring down enemies like they owe him money. But here's the rub: Momoa's charisma is a double-edged sword. He can carry a scene with a single glance, but if the script leans too hard on his physicality—shirtless warrior, anyone?—it risks turning his character into a stereotype rather than a fully realized leader. I'm rooting for him to flex his dramatic range, not just his biceps, and show us the vulnerability of a man caught between duty and doubt.

The supporting cast, while less spotlighted in the trailer, looks like a solid mix of fresh faces and seasoned players. Names like Temuera Morrison and Cliff Curtis, both Māori actors with serious cred, are rumored to be involved based on industry chatter and X buzz. Morrison, who's basically New Zealand's answer to a national treasure after The Mandalorian and Moana, brings a gravitas that could ground the show's bigger moments. If he's playing an elder or rival chief, as some speculate, his quiet intensity could be the perfect foil to Momoa's fire. Curtis, known for Whale Rider and Once Were Warriors, has a knack for stealing scenes with understated power, and I'm hoping he gets meaty material to work with. The trailer also teases a female lead—possibly Luciane Buchanan, another name floating around—who appears in glimpses as a fierce, composed figure. If she's Momoa's ally or adversary, her chemistry with him could make or break the emotional core. The ensemble's rounded out by lesser-known Hawaiian actors, which is a smart move. Casting locals, as Momoa's pushed for per X posts, adds authenticity and gives the show a chance to elevate new talent, but it's a gamble if the newcomers can't hold their own against heavyweights.

The big question is whether this cast can gel into something more than a Momoa showcase. The trailer's focus on him is understandable—he's the draw—but a historical epic needs a deep bench to feel alive. Think Gladiator: Russell Crowe was the star, but Joaquin Phoenix and Oliver Reed made that world feel real. If Chief of War gives its supporting players room to breathe, it could create a rich, lived-in Hawaii where every character feels essential. But if it's just Momoa doing the heavy lifting while everyone else stands around looking intense, it'll feel like a one-man show with great scenery. Early word on X suggests the cast spent time immersing in Hawaiian culture—language, hula, history—which is promising. That kind of prep could mean performances that feel rooted, not just actors playing dress-up.

There's also the wildcard of Momoa's off-screen role. As a co-creator, he's got skin in the game, but that can cut both ways. His passion could elevate the performances, ensuring everyone's dialed in, or it could lead to a show that's too much his vision, sidelining other voices. The trailer's energy suggests he's pouring everything into this, but I'm curious if the ensemble gets enough spotlight to shine. This cast has the potential to be a knockout, but they'll need a script that gives them more to do than look epic in slow motion. For now, Momoa's the sun, and the rest are orbiting—here's hoping they all get a chance to burn bright.

Chapter 3

Direction and Cinematography – Painting Hawaii with Grit and Glory

If the trailer for Chief of War is any indication, Apple TV+ is going all-in to make this series look like a love letter to Hawaii, written in blood, sweat, and volcanic ash. Dropping on August 1, 2025, this nine-episode saga has a visual swagger that's hard to ignore—think sweeping landscapes meeting brutal battle scenes, all under the guiding hand of its directors and cinematographers. But does the direction have the focus to tell a cohesive story, and is the cinematography more than just a pretty postcard? Let's break down how Chief of War aims to capture the soul of 18th-century Hawaii through its lens and leadership, with a few side-eyes at potential pitfalls.

The direction, helmed by a team that includes names like Thomas Pa'a Sibbett (a Hawaiian filmmaker with a knack for cultural storytelling, per X buzz) and possibly a big-name guest director or two, has a massive job: balancing a historical epic's scale with intimate human moments. The trailer suggests they're leaning hard into the former, with shots of warriors charging through jungles and tense standoffs under stormy skies. Momoa's role as co-creator likely gives him a say in the director's chair, and you can feel his influence in the trailer's raw energy—every frame pulses with a sense of urgency, like the islands themselves are characters in the story. But directing a show like this is like herding wild boars: you've got to wrangle big action, cultural nuance, and character depth without losing the thread. The trailer's pacing is relentless, which is thrilling but raises a red flag. Will the directors slow down enough to let quieter moments—like a warrior grappling with doubt or a village mourning a loss—breathe? If they lean too hard on spectacle, Chief of War could feel like a theme park ride: fun, flashy, but forgettable.

Cinematography, though, is where this show might just steal your breath. The trailer's visuals, likely shot by a pro like Greig Fraser (who did Dune, and there's chatter on X he might be involved), are a masterclass in making Hawaii the star. From emerald valleys to jagged cliffs kissed by ocean spray, every frame screams "this is worth your Apple TV+ subscription." The color palette is rich but grounded—think deep greens and fiery oranges, not the oversaturated Instagram filter vibe of lesser epics. Battle scenes are chaotic yet clear, with dynamic camera work that puts you in the thick of it without resorting to shaky-cam nonsense. There's a standout shot in the trailer where a lone figure stands on a cliff at dawn, silhouetted against a glowing sky— it's the kind of image that sticks with you, promising a story as epic as the landscape. The use of natural light, especially in night scenes lit by torches, gives it a tactile, lived-in feel that CGI-heavy shows often miss.

But here's where I get skeptical. Gorgeous visuals are great, but they can't save a story that's running on fumes. The trailer's so packed with eye candy—slow-mo spear throws, misty mountains—that I worry the cinematography might outshine the narrative. Historical dramas like The Last Kingdom work because the visuals serve the story, not the other way around. If Chief of War's directors and DPs get too caught up in making every shot a painting, they risk turning it into a two-hour screensaver. There's also the question of cultural authenticity. X posts from Hawaiian users praise the show's commitment to local talent and locations, but if the direction leans too Hollywood—think overly choreographed battles that feel like a

Marvel movie—it could dilute the Hawaiian heart Momoa's pushing for. The trailer's got a few shots that feel a tad polished, like they're aiming for Emmy voters rather than raw truth.

Still, the potential is sky-high. The directors seem to know when to go big (epic battles) and when to pull back (a close-up of Momoa's weathered face). The cinematography's use of Hawaii's natural beauty—shot on location, per industry reports—gives it an edge over studio-bound epics. If the team can balance the grandeur with grit, letting the visuals amplify the story rather than overshadow it, Chief of War could be a visual triumph. For now, the trailer's got me hyped, but I'm keeping my fingers crossed that the direction doesn't let the scenery steal the show.

Chapter 4

Music and Soundtrack – Drumming Up the Soul of Hawaii

When you hit play on the Chief of War trailer, the first thing that grabs you isn't just the lush Hawaiian vistas or Momoa's intense scowl—it's the sound. A deep, pulsing drumbeat kicks in, layered with eerie chants and the faint crash of waves, like the islands themselves are whispering to you. Set to premiere on August 1, 2025, on Apple TV+, this nine-episode saga is banking on its soundtrack to bring 18th-century Hawaii to life, and if the trailer's any clue, the music is aiming to be as much a character as the warriors on screen. But can the score and sound design match the show's ambition, or will it fall into the trap of generic epic vibes? Let's crank up the volume and see what's humming beneath the surface.

The trailer's soundscape, likely a teaser of the full soundtrack, is a blend of traditional Hawaiian elements and modern cinematic flair. You've got those bone-rattling drums—probably ipu or pahu, rooted in Hawaiian hula and ritual—mixed with haunting vocal chants that feel like they're calling ancestors into the fight. It's the kind of music that makes your chest thump, setting the stage for battles and betrayals. X posts from fans hype up the involvement of Hawaiian musicians, with names like Kealiʻi Reichel or Hōkū Zuttermeister floating around as possible contributors. If true, that's a smart move. Native artists bring an authenticity that can't be faked, grounding the score in the culture Momoa's so passionate about. The trailer's music doesn't just sound epic; it feels specific, like it's tied to the land and history of Hawaii, not some off-the-shelf "tribal" sound kit.

But here's where I squint a little. Big-budget shows like this can sometimes lean too hard on Hollywood polish, slapping orchestral swells over every dramatic moment until it feels like you're watching a Lord of the Rings knockoff. The trailer avoids that for the most part, keeping things raw with percussion and vocals, but there's a hint of that glossy strings section creeping in during the "heroic" shots. If the full soundtrack goes overboard with generic epic chords, it could dilute the Hawaiian soul. Think Braveheart versus Moana—one's a classic but could be set anywhere, the other's unmistakably tied to its culture. Chief of War needs to lean toward the latter, using instruments like the 'ukulele, nose flute, or even slack-key guitar to keep it rooted. The trailer's sparse use of modern synths is a nice touch, adding tension without overpowering, but I'm hoping the composers—possibly someone like Bear McCreary, who's done Battlestar Galactica and knows how to blend cultural sounds—don't let it tip into sci-fi territory.

Sound design is another beast, and the trailer's got me intrigued. The clank of spears, the rustle of palm fronds, the distant roar of the ocean—it's immersive without being overdone. There's a moment where a war cry cuts through the mix, sharp and raw, and it gave me chills. That kind of attention to detail can make or break a show like this, especially in quiet scenes where the sound of footsteps on volcanic rock or the murmur of a village could pull you deeper into the world. But here's the catch: sound design in historical epics can sometimes get lazy, leaning on stock effects like "generic battle clamor" or "ominous wind." If Chief of War wants to stand out, it needs to make every sound feel like it belongs in 1790s Hawaii, not a soundstage in L.A. X chatter suggests the production team worked with cultural consultants to nail the authenticity, which is promising, but it's gotta carry through in the final mix.

The big question is whether the music and sound can do more than just set the mood. A great soundtrack doesn't just underscore action—it tells the story. Think of The Last of the Mohicans, where the score carried the weight of loss and defiance. If Chief of War's music can weave in themes of identity and resilience, mirroring the show's core, it could elevate the whole experience. But if it's just background noise to make battles feel "cool," it's a missed opportunity. The trailer's got me hopeful, with its blend of cultural depth and cinematic punch, but I'm keeping an ear out for whether the full series delivers a sound that's as unforgettable as Hawaii itself.

Chapter 5

Behind the Scenes – Production Context and Budget: Building a Hawaiian Epic

Making a show like Chief of War is like trying to wrangle a volcano: it's ambitious, expensive, and there's a good chance something's gonna blow up. Set to hit Apple TV+ on August 1, 2025, this nine-episode saga isn't just a passion project for Jason Momoa—it's a logistical beast that's got Apple's deep pockets, a cultural tightrope, and a production crew sweating under the

Hawaiian sun. From location shoots to cultural consultants, the behind-the-scenes story of Chief of War is as epic as the battles it depicts. But how did this show come together, and does its budget match its ambition, or is it just another streaming flex? Let's pull back the curtain and see what's cooking.

First off, the production context screams "big deal." Momoa, who's not just starring but also co-creating and producing, has been hyping this as a love letter to Hawaiian history since the project was greenlit. X posts from him and fans paint a picture of a guy who's all-in, pushing for authenticity in a way Hollywood rarely sees. The show's roots go back to Momoa's desire to tell a native Hawaiian story, set in the late 18th century during the unification of the islands. That's no small feat—historical dramas are a minefield of accuracy versus entertainment, and doing it in Hawaii, with its complex cultural and colonial history, ups the stakes. Apple TV+, fresh off splashy hits like Ted Lasso and Pachinko, saw this as a chance to flex their prestige-drama muscle, and they're not skimping. Filming on location in Hawaii—Oahu and Maui, per industry reports—is a bold move. It's not just about pretty beaches; it's about grounding the story in the land itself, from volcanic cliffs to sacred heiau sites.

Now, let's talk money. While exact figures are hush-hush, the buzz on X and trade outlets like Variety peg Chief of War as one of Apple's priciest bets yet, with a budget likely north of $15-20 million per episode. That's House of the Dragon territory, folks. The cash is splashed on everything: location shoots, elaborate sets (think recreated Hawaiian villages), and a small army of cultural consultants to ensure the costumes, language, and rituals don't feel like a tourist brochure. Momoa's involvement as a producer means he's got a hand in where those dollars go, and early reports suggest a chunk went to hiring local talent—actors, crew, even hula experts—to keep it real. But here's where I raise an eyebrow: big budgets don't always mean big quality. Apple's got a history of throwing money at shows (cough The Morning Show cough) that look great but feel hollow if the story's weak. If Chief of War spent millions on CGI waves or overblown battle scenes at the expense of a tight script, it could end up a gorgeous dud.

The production wasn't all smooth sailing. X chatter mentions challenges like weather—Hawaii's rain and heat don't play nice with tight schedules—and the logistical nightmare of filming during a global push for sustainable sets. Apple's been vocal about eco-friendly production, but building massive sets in remote locations while keeping the carbon footprint low? That's a tall order. Then there's the cultural pressure. Momoa's been open about working with Hawaiian elders and historians to get the details right, from war chants to canoe designs. That's a win, but it's also a risk—if the show feels too didactic, like it's trying to teach rather than tell a story, it could alienate viewers who just want a gripping drama. On the flip side, if it leans too Hollywood, it risks pissing off the very community it's meant to honor. The production team's walking a tightrope, and you can bet Momoa's out there with a megaphone, making sure they don't fall.

What's exciting is the local impact. Hiring Hawaiian crew members and involving native artisans isn't just good PR—it's a chance to boost an industry that's often overshadowed by mainland studios. But big budgets and good intentions don't guarantee success. The production's scale could mean stunning visuals and authentic details, or it could mean a bloated mess where every dollar shows but the heart gets lost. The trailer's polish suggests Apple's not cutting corners, but I'm hoping the budget went to storytelling as much as spectacle. For now, Chief of War's behind-the-scenes hustle looks like a labor of love with a side of corporate cash—here's hoping it erupts into something unforgettable.

Chapter 6

Streaming Success – Expected Returns and Audience Appeal: Will Hawaii Conquer the Algorithm?

In the wild world of streaming, where every platform's fighting for your eyeballs like warriors over the last slice of pizza, Chief of War is Apple TV+'s big swing for summer 2025. Dropping on August 1, this nine-episode epic, with Jason Momoa as its spear-wielding poster boy, is poised to make waves—or wipe out spectacularly. With a hefty budget and a cultural hook, the show's got the ingredients for a hit, but will it pull in the viewers and justify Apple's cash splash? Let's break down its streaming potential, who's likely to hit play, and whether it can stand out in a sea of algorithm-driven binges, all while keeping the snark high and spoilers low.

First, let's talk numbers—well, the speculative kind, since Apple guards its streaming stats like a dragon hoarding gold. Chief of War's rumored $15-20 million per episode price tag puts it in the same league as Stranger Things or The Rings of Power. Apple's betting big, and they'll want a return that goes beyond critical pats on the back. The trailer's racked up solid views on YouTube, and X posts show Momoa's fanbase—plus Hawaiian locals and history nerds—hyping it like it's the second coming of Game of Thrones. Apple's platform thrives on prestige dramas, and Chief of War fits the bill: a visually stunning, culturally rich story that screams "Emmy bait." If it lands in the top 10 on Apple's charts (they don't share exact numbers, but we know hits like Ted Lasso dominate), it could drive subscriptions, especially with Momoa's global pull. Posts on X suggest international fans, from Australia to Brazil, are stoked for a non-Western epic, which could give it a broader reach than your average period drama.

But here's the catch: streaming success isn't just about views—it's about buzz and retention. Apple TV+ isn't Netflix; it's got a smaller subscriber base, so Chief of War needs to hook new sign-ups and keep them from canceling post-binge. The trailer's cinematic vibe and Momoa's star power are catnip for action fans and his Aquaman crowd, but the historical setting might scare off viewers who prefer zombies or spaceships. The show's cultural authenticity—pushed hard by Momoa, per X—is a double-edged sword. It could draw in audiences craving diverse stories, especially Pacific Islander and Indigenous communities, but if it feels too "educational," it risks losing the popcorn crowd. Apple's marketing, leaning on Momoa's charisma and Hawaii's beauty, is smart, but they'll need to sell the drama, not just the scenery. A viral moment—like a killer battle clip or a Momoa interview going wild on X—could tip the scales.

Who's this for? The audience appeal splits a few ways. First, you've got Momoa's diehards—fans who'd watch him read a phone book if it was set in Hawaii. They're a lock. Then there's the historical drama buffs, the ones who binged Vikings and Shogun and want a fresh take on a lesser-known era. The Hawaiian and Pacific Islander diaspora, as seen in X posts praising the show's cultural focus, will likely show up in droves, especially if word spreads about its authenticity. But here's where I get skeptical: will it grab the casual streamer, the one scrolling Apple TV+ after Silo and wondering if this is worth nine hours? The trailer's intense, but if the show leans too heavy on historical context or slow-burn character arcs, it could lose the "just entertain me" crowd. Apple's got a chance to broaden its appeal by pushing the action and romance angles—Momoa brooding opposite a fierce co-star could be meme gold—but they'll need to balance that with the cultural weight.

The competition's fierce. By August 2025, Netflix, Amazon, and HBO will be slinging their own heavyweights, and Chief of War needs to cut through the noise. If it delivers a gripping story with universal stakes—think betrayal and heroism over history lessons—it could be a word-of-mouth hit. But if it's too niche or gets lost in its own ambition, it might fade like so many streaming also-rans. The X hype is strong, and Apple's got the cash to push it, but success hinges on keeping viewers hooked past episode one.

For now, Chief of War looks like a contender, but it's gotta fight for its throne in the streaming wars.

Conclusion

A Hawaiian Epic Poised to Soar

or Stumble

As we stand on the edge of Chief of War's premiere on August 1, 2025, it's clear Apple TV+ is swinging for the fences with this one. This nine-episode saga, with Jason Momoa as its beating heart, has all the makings of a game-changer: a fresh take on a rarely explored slice of history, a cast that blends star power with local talent, visuals that could make you book a flight to Hawaii, and a soundtrack that thumps like a war drum. But for every reason to get hyped, there's a question mark. Can the story match the spectacle? Will the cultural authenticity shine without feeling like a lecture? Is this Momoa's triumph or just another streaming giant flexing its wallet?

The plot promises a gritty dive into 18th-century Hawaii, wrestling with themes of identity, leadership, and survival that could hit hard if the writing's sharp. Momoa's charisma anchors a cast that's got potential to steal scenes, but they'll need room to shine beyond his shadow. The direction and cinematography look like a love letter to the islands, though I'm crossing my fingers they don't let the pretty shots outshine the heart.

The music's got that raw, cultural pulse, but it needs to stay true to Hawaii and not go full Hollywood. Behind the scenes, the production's ambition—fueled by a massive budget and Momoa's passion—shows commitment, but big bucks don't always mean big wins. And in the streaming wars, Chief of War has to fight for eyeballs against a flood of competitors, banking on its unique setting and universal stakes to pull in both history nerds and casual bingers.

What's the bottom line? Chief of War is a bold bet, one that could redefine how we tell epic stories or trip over its own lofty goals. It's got the tools to be unforgettable—a star with heart, a setting that's a character in itself, and a cultural mission that feels personal. But it's walking a tightrope between authentic and overproduced, gripping and generic. As the premiere looms, I'm rooting for it to land as a story that's as powerful as a Hawaiian sunrise, not just another pretty wave that crashes and fades. Whether it's a knockout or a near-miss, Chief of War is about to make some noise—here's hoping it's the kind that echoes.

Final Verdict

Who'll Love It and What's It Worth?

Chief of War is for Momoa fans who'd follow him into a volcano, historical drama buffs craving a fresh angle, and anyone who loves a story where culture and conflict collide. Pacific Islander audiences and those hungry for authentic, non-Western epics will likely eat it up, especially if the show nails its Hawaiian soul. Casual streamers might hesitate if it's too heavy, but action-packed battles and Momoa's charm could hook them. It's not for those who want light fluff or sci-fi escapism—this one demands attention.

Rating: 8/10 (speculative, based on potential). It's got the makings of a banger, but I'm docking points for the risk of style over substance. If it balances heart and spectacle, it could climb higher.

Bibliography

Chief of War Official Trailer. YouTube, uploaded by Apple TV, 2025, https://youtu.be/owdGcwufWK8?si=4J1SaY X2QoCl7Jr6.

Various X posts by Jason Momoa and fans, discussing Chief of War production and cultural significance, accessed July 29, 2025.

Industry reports from Variety and Deadline on Apple TV+'s 2025 slate and Chief of War budget estimates, accessed July 29, 2025. General web information on Hawaiian history and cultural consultants involved in Chief of War, accessed July 29, 2025.

Made in the USA
Columbia, SC
09 September 2025